SUSAN MEDDAUGH

Cinderella's Rat

HOUGHTON MIFFLIN COMPANY BOSTON 1997

In memory of
Frisky and Wiley—
great rats!

Walter Lorraine (wʌ) Books

Copyright © 1997 by Susan Meddaugh

For information about this and other Houghton Mifflin trade
and reference books and multimedia products, visit The Bookstore
at Houghton Mifflin on the World Wide Web at
http://www.hmco.com/trade/ .

Library of Congress Cataloging-in-Publication Data

Meddaugh, Susan.
Cinderella's rat / Susan Meddaugh.
        p.   cm.
Summary: One of the rats that was turned into a coachman by
Cinderella's fairy godmother tells his story.
ISBN 0-395-86833-5
[1. Rats–Fiction. 2. Brothers and sisters–Fiction.
3. Characters in literature–Fiction.] I. Title.
PZ7.M51273Ci 1997
[E]--dc21   97-2156
                                                 CIP
                                                  AC

Printed in the United States of America
WOZ 10 9 8 7 6 5 4 3 2 1

I was born a rat.
I expected to be a rat all my days.

But life is full of surprises.

Being a rat is no picnic.
Cats are plentiful and food is scarce.

My sister Ruth and I were always hungry.
One day hunger drove us to do a foolish thing...

and we were caught!

A rat in a trap has usually enjoyed his last bite of cheese.
Ruth and I huddled together as the trap door was opened.

Then we jumped for our lives.
That's when it happened.

Something

was

rearranging

 my

parts.

I became a COACHMAN.

Well, more of a coachboy.

An old woman spoke sternly to me:
"Take this girl to the castle."
To the girl she said,
"Don't forget to be home by midnight."

When we got to the castle the girl ran off to the ball.
Kitchen smells drew me like a magnet.
"Make yourself useful, boy!" said the cook. "Bring me
some flour from the larder."

Rat heaven!

I dove into an open bag of grain.
"You must be *really* hungry!" said a voice behind me.
A boy was standing in the doorway.

"It tastes better like this," he said. And to my surprise,
he handed me a hunk of bread. We sat and ate, side by side.

Suddenly the boy leaped to his feet.
"A RAT!" he shouted. "KILL IT!"
"He knows!" I thought, and covered my head to protect myself.
But the boy wasn't looking at me.

As he raised his foot, I saw a familiar face.

The truth was out.

"This is the end of us," I thought.

Finally the boy spoke.

"That must have been some powerful magic spell to turn your sister into a rat," he said. "Come. What we need is a wizard."

We stepped out into the night.

At the wizard's cottage, the boy asked the wizard to change
my sister back into a girl. I was hopelessly confused. If
I explained the *real* problem, the wizard would turn us both
into food for cats.

Maybe Ruth would like being a girl.

The wizard started to chant.

"Eye of newt and tooth of bat,
magic brighter than a pearl.
Take away this loathsome rat
and give us back a pretty...

…CAT?"

"No!" I cried. "Change her back!"
"Surely a cat is better than a rat," said the boy.
"Not where I come from," I said.

The wizard tried again.

"Eye of bat and tooth of newt,
magic beebleberry root.
Now I give my wand a twirl.
Give us, please, a lovely…

...GIRL!"

"That's better," said the wizard.
"Much better!" said the boy.
 My sister said...

The wizard prepared another potion.

"Forty feathers of a quail,
magic salamander tail,
wing of bee and toe of gnat,
take away this voice of cat."

The wizard was tired.
"It's almost midnight," he said. "Come back tomorrow
and I'll try again."

So the three of us wandered back to the castle, where we all said goodnight. As I climbed onto the coach, a clock began to chime. At the stroke of twelve, once again…

my parts started to come and go

changing

and

rearranging...

until at last I was ME.

But...

Now I live in a cottage with my family.
Food is plentiful

and cats are scarce.

Life is full of surprises, so you may as well get used to it.

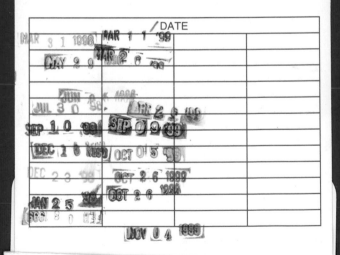